RAINBOW magic

SPECIAL EDITION

TRIXIE
THE HALLOWEEN FAIRY

By Daisy Meadows

Illustrated by Georgie Ripper

Silver Dolphin

Silver Dolphin Books

An imprint of Printers Row Publishing Group
A division of Readerlink Distribution Services, LLC
9717 Pacific Heights Blvd, San Diego, CA 92121
www.silverdolphinbooks.com

ISBN: 978-1-6672-0384-3
Manufactured, printed, and assembled in Guangzhou, China.
First printing, February 2023. GD/02/23
27 26 25 24 23   1 2 3 4 5

Table of Contents

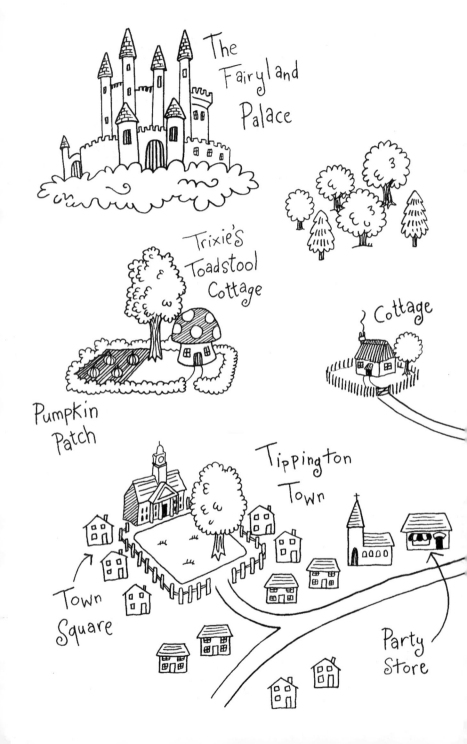

I, Jack Frost, have planned a nasty scare.
Indeed, all humans should beware.
This year, Halloween will be all trick—no treat,
Since my goblins stole what makes the day so sweet.

To the world of humans the goblins go.
The magic candy is lost and must stay so.
All kids in costume will have a mighty fright,
When they have no fun on Halloween night!

Find the hidden letters in the pumpkins
throughout this book. Unscramble all
twelve letters to spell a special Halloween
phrase! See page 161 for the answer.

BOOK ONE

THE CHOCOLATE BAR CHASE

TABLE OF CONTENTS

BUTTONS
BARKS

"I can't wait to show you the fairy wings," Rachel Walker said to her best friend, Kirsty Tate, as they climbed the stairs to Rachel's room.

"I'm excited to see them," Kirsty replied. "It will be so much fun to trick-or-treat together!"

Kirsty was visiting Rachel while her parents were out of town, and it just happened to be Halloween weekend! They were both going to dress up as fairies.

The two girls exchanged smiles as Rachel lifted the lid of a storage box. Inside were two sets of glittery fairy wings: one was pale pink and the other was a light purple.

"Oh, Rachel! They look almost real,"
Kirsty said, giving her friend a knowing
look. After all, the girls knew just how
real fairies' wings looked. They were
friends with the fairies!

Rachel and Kirsty met during vacation
with their families on beautiful Rainspell
Island. There, they had helped the
Rainbow Fairies get back to Fairyland
after they had been banished by wicked
Jack Frost. Since then, the girls had
helped lots of fairies. Now the king and
queen of Fairyland looked to
them whenever Jack Frost
was up to his old tricks.

"I'm going to try
mine on," Kirsty said,
carefully lifting up
a sparkly set of wings.

Just then, they heard a loud bark. Buttons, Rachel's adorable sheepdog, raced into the room. He knocked into Kirsty and tore through the storage box on his way to the window.

"Buttons!" Rachel yelled as the costumes flew up in the air. But Buttons kept barking at something outside. Then he turned to Rachel and whimpered. "What is it, boy?" Rachel asked with concern.

"Oh! There's a kitten in the tree!" Kirsty said, pointing out the window. The kitten was black from its nose to its tail.

"That's strange," Rachel said. "Buttons usually loves cats."

Now the big sheepdog pawed at the window.

"Do you think the kitten's stuck?" Kirsty asked. "Maybe it needs our help."

But at that moment, the little black cat leaped onto a nearby branch. It strutted past the window and seemed to look right at Buttons and the girls, then scurried down another tree.

Buttons let out a yelp, dashed from the room, and ran down the stairs.

"Weird," Rachel said with a laugh.

Kirsty nodded before letting out a groan. "Oh no! Look at our costumes!"

Rachel bent down and lifted up her wings. The thin fabric had big tears in it. Kirsty's wings looked the same.

"It must have happened when Buttons raced through here. His nails are so sharp!"

"But that's not all that's wrong," Kirsty said, glancing around. "The glitter seems to have fallen

off the fabric. The wings aren't shimmery anymore. And it looks like one of our wands is missing."

"I can't see my fun fairy tights, either," Rachel added, looking around the room and under her bed. She sat up and sighed.

"It looks like there may be something mysterious going on here," Kirsty said.

"Mysterious or magical?" Rachel whispered.

Kirsty's eyes sparkled. She hoped her friend was right!

"Either way, I guess we'll have to start over with our fairy costumes."

"Let's go to the costume and craft store to pick up some supplies," Rachel suggested. "We only have two days left until Halloween!"

COSTUME CHAOS

Rachel and Kirsty made a list of what they needed at the costume store and grabbed their bags. Then Rachel told her mom where they were going.

As they walked down the street, the girls wondered what had happened to the other parts of their costumes. "It doesn't make sense," Kirsty said. "I remember seeing two wands in the box."

Rachel shrugged her shoulders. "I don't
know, either," she said. "But I'm sure we'll
find everything we need at Costumes,
Cauldrons, and Crafts. It's the best
Halloween store. I know the owner,
Mrs. Burns. She has all kinds
of fairy stuff."

The girls walked
toward the center of
town. The sun was
out, and the air was
cool and crisp.
"It feels like it's
almost Halloween,"
Kirsty said, pulling
gloves from her
pocket. "And, look!
That looks just like a
haunted house!"

Rachel knew exactly which house her friend meant. It was a spooky three-story Victorian mansion with lots of windows. The house sat at the end of a long driveway that was lined with crooked trees. "Don't worry," Rachel assured Kirsty. "It's just an old house that nobody has lived in for years. There are stories that it's haunted, but they aren't true."

Just then, Rachel looked at the third-floor window and thought she saw someone there.

"Kirsty!" she exclaimed, but the figure disappeared before she could say more. "Oh, never mind." Rachel tried to pretend that she'd made a mistake, but she didn't think she had imagined it.

When they came to the town square, the girls noticed lots of other people heading for the costume store.

"It's always busy this time of year," Rachel explained, pulling the door open.

But she gasped when she looked around the crowded store.

Parents and kids were everywhere, and they all looked upset. There was a long

line behind a sign that read "RETURNS."

Two grumpy mothers in the line were peering into their bags.

"My son's astronaut costume has bunny ears instead of an oxygen helmet," one complained, shaking her head.

"I bought a ballerina outfit, but it has fireman boots instead of ballet shoes," the other responded.

"All of those people bought
costumes that are mixed up?"
Kirsty whispered
in disbelief.

"I guess so," Rachel
responded. "There's
Mrs. Burns," she said,
pointing to a woman
carrying a straw basket. But
the storeowner didn't notice
the girls. She was too busy rushing around,
clicking her tongue with concern as she
looked at the jumbled shelves.

As the friends walked toward the back of
the store, all the customers were grumbling.
No one could find anything. The girls passed
a group of boys who were digging through
a bin of hats and wigs, trying things on and
throwing them into the air with loud grunts.

No wonder the shop is such a mess,
Kirsty thought.

Just then, Rachel stopped. "This is
where the fairy stuff always is," she said,
pointing to a nearby shelf, "but it's not
here now."

"And what *is* here is all mixed up,"
Kirsty noted as she looked at a parrot mask
with a long, gray trunk instead of a beak.

Next, she picked up a pretty, purple
cone-shaped princess hat. But instead of
having ribbons flowing from the pointy
top, there were rubber snakes with
wagging red tongues.

"Yuck," Rachel declared.

"You can say that again," a twinkling voice sang out.

With that, a burst of star-shaped sparkles filled the air, and a tiny fairy flew out from behind the princess hat. The fairy wore a short and swingy orange dress with a silky black sash, and black-and-orange striped tights.

A star pendant hung around her neck, and she had a mischievous grin.

"You must be Rachel and Kirsty," the fairy said. "I'm Trixie the Halloween Fairy. I need your help!"

THREE TREATS

Rachel and Kirsty gasped in surprise.
They couldn't take their eyes off the
tiny fairy's glittery wings, which were
especially sparkly in the dim store.

"It's nice to meet you," Rachel and
Kirsty said at once. They loved meeting
new fairies!

"And it's a pleasure meeting you,
too. You're pretty famous in Fairyland,"
Trixie said.

The girls smiled at each other. "Trixie, what's wrong?" Kirsty asked, her smile fading. "Why do you need our help?"

Trixie sighed. Her smile quickly fell into a frown. "Halloween is in terrible trouble."

"What happened?" Rachel asked.

Trixie sighed once again. "It all started yesterday," the fairy began. "I had just finished making my magic Halloween candy. Every year, I make three kinds of candy: chocolate bars, candy corn, and caramel apples." The fairy paused and licked her lips.

"Oh, where was I?" she asked herself. "Ah, yes. I sprinkle one piece of candy from each batch with my special star-shaped fairy dust.

These three enchanted pieces of candy
hold the Halloween magic! Without them,
Halloween wouldn't be the same."

"Did something happen to the candy?"
Kirsty asked.

"It's missing!" Trixie cried. Kirsty and
Rachel listened closely. Trixie
told them that each piece of
candy had an important job:
The chocolate bar helped
make sure everyone had a
costume and looked festive.
The magic candy corn's job
was to make sure there was
plenty of candy for everyone
and that it tasted extra sweet.
Finally, the caramel apple helped boost the
Halloween spirit—it let everyone enjoy
the magic of the holiday.

"I wrap each magic piece of candy in an orange glitter wrapper," Trixie added with a twinkle in her eye. "The king and queen give them away as prizes at our Halloween Ball."

"Wow! I didn't even know you celebrated Halloween in Fairyland," Kirsty said.

"Oh, yes," Trixie replied. "We love Halloween! It's one of the few days that people in the human world believe in the magic that lives in Fairyland all year long." Then Trixie scowled a little. "Except Jack Frost. He doesn't want humans to have all of the fun. This year, he came up with a nasty plan."

Trixie explained that she was watering her pumpkin patch when she heard a big racket.

"Oh no," Kirsty said, biting her lip.

"You guessed it," said Trixie, crossing her arms.

The fairy's eyes were serious as she told them about Jack Frost's goblins, who had sneaked into her toadstool cottage to steal the magic candies.

"They were almost to the edge of the
Fairyland Forest when I spotted them—
seven green goblins with chocolate
smeared on their hands and faces. Just as
I lifted my wand to stop them, Jack Frost
appeared. The icy lightning bolts from his
wand crashed into my star sparkles, and
the goblins disappeared in a cloudy haze.
My magic candy was gone too!"

"Oh no! We have to get it back!"
Rachel cried. She couldn't imagine
Halloween without costumes, candy, and
lots of fun.

"Thank you!" Trixie said with a grateful
smile. "But there's just one more thing."
The fairy's deep brown eyes grew wide.
"We can't let the candy fall into the wrong
hands. If someone who doesn't believe
in Halloween eats a piece, that part of
Halloween will be ruined."

Rachel and Kirsty gulped.

Just then, one of the noisy boys who
had been rummaging through the hat
bins stomped his feet. "It's not here!" he
whined. "I'm looking somewhere else."
The others followed, all wearing a hat or
piece of shiny jewelry.

"Did you see that?" Kirsty asked.

"It's awful," Trixie said, shaking her head. "Those boys certainly don't have any real Halloween spirit."

"And they didn't have any shoes!" Rachel blurted out. "But they did have big, green feet."

"Exactly," Kirsty agreed. "Trixie, I think we've found the goblins!"

GOBLINS ON THE GO

Kirsty, Rachel, and Trixie rushed after the goblins.

"They went in there!" Rachel said, pointing at a door with a sign that read STORAGE ROOM.

"Then we have to go in there, too," Trixie announced. She pointed her wand, and the door opened with a burst of star sparkles.

"Trixie!" Kirsty gasped. "You have to be more careful. Someone might see you!"

Trixie quickly flew into Kirsty's pocket until they were safe inside the storage room, which was almost as big as the store itself. There was row after row of shelves, each piled high with boxes—but no sign of goblins.

"Mrs. Burns always has a basket of candy on the counter," Rachel whispered. "Maybe she keeps her candy in here."

"And maybe the glitter chocolate bar is with it!" Trixie declared.

40

The girls had to tiptoe around open costume boxes that littered the floor.

"This room is as messy as the store," Kirsty commented.

"It's because the glitter chocolate bar is missing," Trixie explained. "Everything that has do with costumes is all mixed up."

"That's what happened to our wings!" Rachel said.

"And the other wand," Kirsty added.

Realizing it was safe, Trixie zoomed out of Kirsty's pocket. "Let's go find those goblins and my candy!" she declared.

The girls raced after the fairy, dodging piles of costumes as they went.

When they saw blasts of icy sparks in the next aisle, they slowed down and peeked around the corner.

"Jack Frost gave them a wand," Trixie said. "You have to be careful. It can mix up anything!"

A goblin with extra pointy ears held the wand. He aimed it at a tall goblin dressed as a policeman.

"I want to be the policeman!" he yelled, but the goblin in the policeman costume just shook his head. Just then, icy bolts shot from the other goblin's wand, and the policeman's blue uniform shirt changed to a sparkly yellow halter top.

"Change it back!" yelped the tall goblin, blowing on his police whistle.

"No!" the pointy-eared goblin refused, then aimed the wand again and a ferocious dragon costume suddenly turned bright pink with purple flowers.

"That explains the mismatched costumes," Kirsty whispered.

The other goblins were pulling down boxes and ripping through them.

"They must think one of the magic candies is here," Trixie guessed.

At that moment, Kirsty thought she saw a flash of something orange and glittery. "They've found a piece of candy!" Kirsty yelled, not able to control her excitement. "It must be the chocolate bar. Let's get it!"

As soon as the goblins heard Kirsty, they stopped what they were doing and raced toward the back door.

Hot on the goblins' trail, the girls ran through the door and into the alley with Trixie flying overhead. As they chased the goblins around the corner, they searched for another glimpse of the glitter wrapper. The seven goblins were running in a mob, dropping wigs and hats wherever they went.

"Oh no! They're heading for the town square," Rachel said as the goblins made their way across Main Street and onto the grassy area in the center of the village.

Trixie and the girls looked around frantically. They couldn't let anyone else spot the goblins! The three friends were gaining on the goblin gang, but they still had no idea which one had the magic candy.

All at once, a black cat sprung out of a tree and pounced down in the middle of the goblins' path.

"Yikes!" screeched the first goblin as he tripped and fell. When he tried to get up, another goblin toppled over him, then another, until they were all in a giant heap.

"It's the little black cat!" Rachel said, watching the kitten climb from the bottom of the goblin pile. It seemed to look at the girls and Trixie before bounding across the park and out of sight.

"And here's our orange glitter," said Kirsty. She sounded disappointed as she picked up something from the ground. "It isn't a magic candy wrapper at all." The orange glitter was on a tiger mask that a goblin had taken from the storage room. "Now we have to start all over."

"Don't worry, Trixie, we'll find the magic candies," Rachel said, but when she looked around, she didn't see Trixie anywhere.

Where had their fairy friend gone?

LOST AND FOUND

The girls walked quickly away from the goblins, who were still in a jumble, and started searching for Trixie. At once, the fairy zipped down from high in the sky.

"Did you find something?" Rachel asked hopefully.

"Not really," Trixie responded. "I was looking for Moonlight."

"Moonlight?" Kirsty asked, shielding her eyes as she glanced up at the sunny sky.

"The little black kitten," Trixie replied with a small smile. "He must have gotten mixed up in the spells that sent the magic candy into the human world."

"Is he your kitten?" Rachel asked.

"Not really. He's been hanging around my cottage in Fairyland ever since I started making my Halloween candy," the fairy explained. "He's kind of shy, very spunky, and he seems to have a sweet tooth."

"We saw him this morning, too," Kirsty said. "At Rachel's house."

"I hope he doesn't get lost in the human world.

I'm sure the king and queen would want me to take him back to Fairyland, but we have to find the magic candy first," Trixie said.

Kirsty and Rachel knew they only had two days until Halloween, and they still needed to find all three pieces of magical candy!

The three friends headed back to the costume shop. Along the way, they picked up the costumes that the goblins had dropped in their mad dash from the storage room.

"If the orange glitter were really just a tiger mask, the magic chocolate bar could still be at Costumes, Caldrons, and Crafts," Kirsty said.

"Or somewhere else," Rachel admitted.

"We should trust that the magic will come to us," Trixie reminded them. The queen of Fairyland often gave the girls that same advice.

When they arrived back at the store, Mrs. Burns was trying to clean up the mess. "I just don't understand what happened," she said. "I don't like it when people are unhappy with their costumes. I can't even find the candy that I had to give away. It doesn't feel like Halloween at all!"

Still, the storeowner smiled when she saw Rachel.

As soon as Mrs. Burns heard that Rachel and Kirsty needed supplies for their fairy costumes, she hurried off to find wings and other things.

"Let's help pick up," Rachel suggested.

Kirsty, Rachel, and Trixie went to the back of the store and started to put things back in the right place. When no one was looking, Trixie used her wand to send sticks of makeup and trick-or-treat bags back on the shelves with a sparkle. In no time, the floors were clean and the bins were almost full.

"If we don't find new wings, I could always be a clown," Rachel said with a laugh as she picked up a bright red clown wig. As she plopped it on her head, candy came showering down out of the wig and landed in a heap on the floor.

"Look!" Kirsty exclaimed, pointing to a glittery orange wrapper at the top of the pile.

"Oh, Rachel!" Mrs. Burns said, rushing forward. "You found our trick-or-treat candy! And I just happen to have the basket right here!"

Kirsty held her breath as the storeowner bent down to gather the candy.

Immediately, the girls kneeled down to help. Rachel gave Kirsty a concerned glance as they watched Mrs. Burns toss the glitter chocolate bar into the straw basket.

"It just hasn't felt like Halloween without our candy basket," Mrs. Burns said, standing up and starting to walk away. Kirsty's face dropped as the woman went around the corner.

"What am I thinking?" Mrs. Burns asked, hurrying back. "Would you like a piece?"

As soon as Mrs. Burns made the offer, Kirsty's hand sprang forward to grab the chocolate bar with the orange glitter wrapper.

"Thank you, Mrs. Burns," she said, beaming. "It does feel more like Halloween already." Kirsty secretly held the candy behind her back, and Trixie swooped down to pick it up.

"And look!" Mrs. Burns declared, pointing to something on the very top shelf. "I can see my favorite fairy wings. I wondered where they were hiding."

The storeowner climbed up the old, rolling ladder to pull the sparkly packages off the shelf. She handed one to Rachel and another to Kirsty. "You girls have been such a help. Please take these as a special thank you."

"Oh, Mrs. Burns, they're beautiful," Rachel said with a delighted sigh.

"Thank you so much," added Kirsty.

As the girls grinned, they saw Trixie swoosh into the air behind Mrs. Burns. The cheery fairy spun around and gave the glittery orange candy a little kiss. Rachel and Kirsty watched her fly away, knowing she was headed back to Fairyland.

"Our costumes are going to look amazing," Rachel said, turning to Kirsty.

"And once Trixie returns the chocolate candy to Fairyland, everyone's costumes will start to come together," agreed Kirsty. "Now we just have two more pieces of candy to track down, and we'll all have a happy Halloween!"

BOOK TWO

THE CANDY CORN CAPER

TABLE OF CONTENTS

All Dressed Up

"Happy Halloween!" Mr. Walker said, snapping a picture of Rachel and Kirsty with his camera. "You look great!"

"Just like real fairies," Rachel's mom added, her hands clasped.

Rachel and Kirsty smiled at each other. They both wore beautiful, glittery wings on their backs. Kirsty had on a short, purple pleated skirt and a lilac wrap sweater with bell sleeves.

Rachel had chosen
a pretty green
sweater dress with
ballerina flats.
A gold locket
shimmered
around each of
their necks. The
lockets had been
gifts from the
king and queen of
Fairyland.

"I wonder where
our newest fairy friend could be," Kirsty
whispered, suddenly concerned. The best
friends had not seen Trixie since they
had found the magic chocolate bar in the
costume store a few days earlier.

Ding-dong! Ding-dong!

"I'll get that," Mr. Walker offered. He put on a cowboy hat to match his jeans and boots as he headed to the front door. Rachel's mom followed him. She wore a matching cowboy hat with a long jean skirt. Her checked shirt was tied at the waist.

"We know Trixie made it to Fairyland with the chocolate bar," Rachel said under her breath. "All of our costumes look amazing! If the chocolate wasn't back in Fairyland, the costumes would still be mixed up."

63

"Trixie will show up soon," Kirsty said with a sigh. "I'm sure of it." It was almost time to trick-or-treat, and they still had to find two more pieces of glitter candy!

Just then, Rachel's dad rushed into the living room. "Girls, do you know where our candy went? It seems to have disappeared. Even the bowl is gone!"

Kirsty and Rachel looked at each other.

"We have no idea where it is," Rachel replied. It was true. They didn't have any idea where the candy was, but they did have an idea of *why* it was missing. It was all because of Jack Frost and his tricky goblins!

"Well, there are a bunch of ghosts at our door, and we don't have anything to give them!" Mr. Walker rushed to the kitchen, his cowboy boots clip-clopping on the floor.

Buttons let out a bark.

"Oh, I forgot how nervous Buttons gets on Halloween," Rachel said, running toward the front door. She got there just in time to grab the woolly sheepdog's collar. "It's okay, boy. He doesn't like all of the costumes," Rachel explained.

The girls looked out the open door into the dusky night. The neighborhood was starting to fill with firemen and superheroes, princesses and knights, dinosaurs and lions. They could see a large group of boys dressed as ghosts scampering down the street.

"Those ghosts didn't even wait for Dad to find the candy," said Rachel.

"And look! There's Trixie's kitten, Moonlight. He's running after the ghosts," Kirsty added with a laugh.

The tiny cat was leaping through the tall grass.

Kirsty lowered her voice to a whisper. "I wonder if those ghosts are actually . . . goblins?" Rachel gasped, her eyes widening.

Just then, Rachel's parents returned to the front hall. Mr. Walker was rubbing his chin. "I guess I'll have to get more candy at the store," he said. "It isn't Halloween without trick-or-treating."

"You two should get going and have fun," suggested Mrs. Walker.

The two best friends grabbed their candy bags and straightened their wings. Kirsty waved as she headed out the door.

"We'll see you at the town party later," Rachel said, giving each of her parents a quick hug.

"Yes, you girls are going to have a busy night!" Mr. Walker replied.

Rachel and Kirsty gave each other worried looks. Little did he know. They still needed to find two more pieces of magic candy—and they were running out of time!

ALL TRICK, NO TREAT

As Kirsty and Rachel headed out to the sidewalk, they saw some older boys walk by.

"Hey! There's a rock in this candy wrapper!" a boy in an alien costume shouted to his friends.

"Yuck! In mine, too!" a boy dressed as a football player sputtered, wiping his mouth on his sleeve. He threw the rock to the ground. "That was a mean trick."

Rachel shook her head and sighed, watching the boys wander away. "I guess we should trick-or-treat," she said, "and see what happens."

"Good idea," agreed Kirsty as they walked up a pebble path. The path led to a house with lots of jack-o'-lanterns placed on the steps. Golden lights flickered through their carved faces with a spooky glow.

"The Kemps live here," Rachel said.

"They're friends with my parents. They always have really good candy."

"I hope *they* can find their candy bowl," Kirsty said, raising her eyebrows.

"Trick or treat!" the girls declared when the door opened.

A woman wearing a crown smiled at them. "Look at you!" Mrs. Kemp said.

Then she paused and called over her shoulder. "Jack, come see the fairies!"

A tall man with thick, white hair appeared behind Mrs. Kemp.

"Are those real wings?" he teased. "You look like you could fly away." Then he held out a basket full of candy for the girls.

73

Rachel and Kirsty looked at each other with surprise. The Kemps had candy after all! There were mini chocolate bars, square fruit chews, round peanut butter cups, and lollipops—nothing in the shape of rocks.

"Thank you, Mr. and Mrs. Kemp!" Rachel exclaimed, choosing a mini chocolate bar. Kirsty took a package of fruit chews.

"Of course," Mrs. Kemp said, waving good-bye. "Now run along and be safe. Happy Halloween!"

"You were right!" Kirsty cried as the girls headed down the stairs. "They did have great stuff! I love fruit chews." Kirsty ripped open the paper wrapper and popped the red candy into her mouth.

At once, her smile dropped and her nose scrunched up. "Rachel," she said, "it doesn't taste good." She paused, moving the candy around in her mouth. "It doesn't taste like anything at all."

Rachel, who had just taken a bite of her chocolate bar, also frowned.

"I know. It's awful!"

The girls immediately looked around, recognizing the voice that echoed through the air. It was Trixie!

The tiny fairy fluttered into view with a cloud of star-shaped fairy dust trailing behind her. The dust sparkled against the dark night sky. "It's because the magic candy corn is still missing," Trixie explained. "The candy corn not only makes sure there is plenty of candy, but it also makes it nice and sweet. We have to find it!"

"Oh, Trixie!" Kirsty cried. "We're so glad to see you!"

"And I'm glad to see you," Trixie replied. "But there's no time to chit-chat. I think I know where the magic candy corn might be!" With that, the little Halloween Fairy whizzed down the street.

A Sweet Clue

Rachel and Kirsty took off, running as fast as they could. They couldn't quite keep up with Trixie. The fairy was dodging trick-or-treaters as she zoomed ahead.

"Someone's going to see her if she's not careful," Rachel said, gasping for breath.

"And she's got to slow down," Kirsty puffed.

Just then, Trixie stopped in midair and looked back at the girls. "This is it!" she called, pointing to a cottage with a stone chimney and tan roof. There was a single candle in the window, and Kirsty could just make out a broom propped up on the porch.

"Come on," Trixie said, grinning and zooming up to the door.

The cottage looked mysterious in the moonlight, but the girls felt safe with Trixie nearby. They climbed up the creaky old porch stairs.

Trixie raised her wand, and a stream of fairy dust pushed the doorbell.

"Trixie, you have to hide!" Rachel insisted, holding open her candy bag. The fairy ducked inside just as the heavy wooden door swung open.

"Trick or treat!" the girls shouted.

A pale face appeared around the edge of the door. The lady had straight black hair and wore a witch's costume. "Of course," she said. "Come pick some candy out of my cauldron."

"Oh no!" the lady exclaimed when she realized the candy was gone. "You're only my second group of trick-or-treaters. I wonder if those rude little ghosts took it all." She bent over and swept her hand through the big iron pot, just to be sure that there was nothing inside. "Even the candy in the pretty glitter wrapper is gone!"

Rachel and Kirsty exchanged glances.

"There were ghosts here before us?" Rachel asked.

"Yes, about six or seven of them. They just left," the lady said, taking off her tall, pointy hat and looking terribly sad. "This is the first Halloween I've had in this house," she added. "I wanted it to be fun."

Kirsty felt awful for her. "We know those ghosts," Kirsty said. "If they took your candy, we'll get it back. Come on, Rachel." Kirsty gave the lady a small smile and a nod. Without another word, she marched down the stairs.

"We're going to find the glitter candy corn," Trixie said, fluttering out of Rachel's candy bag as soon as the girls were out of sight of the cottage. "If that lady is right, the ghosts must have it!"

"So all we have to do is find the ghosts— I mean, goblins," Kirsty replied. "And then all the Halloween candy will be back where it belongs."

"Okay," Rachel agreed. "Where do we start? It's getting dark, so it will be harder to find them. And we don't even know which way they went."

"First of all, I can make your wands a little more useful," Trixie responded. The fairy waved her own wand, and fairy dust swirled around the wands in Kirsty's and Rachel's hands. The wands began to glow

with a bright, silvery light. "And it would help if those wings really worked." With another twirl of Trixie's wand, the girls' wings began to sparkle. As the friends floated up into the air, they shrank down to fairy size.

"That's much better, isn't it?" Trixie declared, her hands on her hips. "Now let's go get those goblins!"

PLAYGROUND GHOSTS

The three fairy friends fluttered their wings until they were high above the trees. "We'll be able to spot that group of ghosts much better from up here," Trixie said.

Kirsty and Rachel flew close behind Trixie. They held their wands in front of them to light the way. They were getting closer to town, and there were more people on the sidewalks and in the streets.

"Hey, look!" Kirsty exclaimed. "I see a bunch of ghosts down there." A streetlight cast a dim glow over the nearby playground. Rachel could just make out a cluster of ghosts hidden in the shadow of a tall tree.

"They have a bunch of baskets of candy!" Trixie declared. "The magic candy corn might be there."

In the cool night, the goblins' voices carried through the air. They were grunting and grumbling as they threw candy and wrappers all around.

Kirsty gasped. "Oh no! They're eating it!" she cried. She remembered that if someone who didn't believe in Halloween ate the magic candy, then that part of Halloween would be ruined.

"What if the goblins ate the magic candy corn?" Kirsty shivered. She couldn't bear to think about Halloween without the taste of rich chocolate, or tangy fruit chews, or sour gummies! "We have to do something, and fast!" she insisted.

"Trixie, can you make us human-size again?" Rachel asked, flying lower in the sky. "We'll have a better chance of catching the goblins on the ground."

"Of course," Trixie said. "But I won't change your wands. You might need the light!"

As soon as Kirsty and Rachel were ready, Trixie waved her wand. The girls took off running toward the goblins the moment their feet touched the grass. "Stop!" they yelled at the same time.

The goblins stopped eating and tried to look around, but they couldn't see through the tiny eyeholes in their white sheets.

"Who was that?" a goblin asked, his voice muffled by the sheet over his head.

"Who cares?" another replied. "Focus! We have to find that magic candy and take it to Jack Frost."

Then a goblin peeked out from under his costume. "Oh no! It's those annoying girls again!" he yelped. "Let's get out of here!"

The goblins scrambled to throw all of the candy back into the baskets, bowls, and bags. Then they stacked them up and tried to balance the towers of treats as they ran toward the street.

"They must have stolen candy from almost every house!" Kirsty said, chasing a goblin with six bowls teetering in his hands.

The goblins stumbled across the playground, barely able to see. One goblin ran right up one side of a seesaw and down the other.

Another got caught on the tire swing. But before the girls knew it, the goblins had made it to the street—and into the middle of the costume parade!

MOONLIGHT'S MAGIC

The street was full of people in costume. Kirsty watched as skeletons and witches and aliens marched by. Then, out of the corner of her eye, Kirsty glimpsed a flash of white. A ghost!

She reached out to grab the ghost's trick-or-treat bag, but then she realized the ghost wore tiny white sneakers.

A goblin could never fit his huge feet into those little shoes, she thought.

Just as she had given up hope, Kirsty felt a tap on her shoulder.

"Look over there," said Rachel, pointing. Kirsty followed her friend's gaze and saw Trixie perched in a tree on the other side of the street. The fairy was waving her arms, and jumping up and down. "Let's go and see what she wants—before anyone else spots her!" Rachel said, grabbing Kirsty's hand and leading her through the crowd of people.

"I'm glad you saw me," Trixie said as she

flew down from the tree and landed on
Rachel's shoulder, "because I spotted the
goblins! They went into that park!"

Rachel and Kirsty peered into the
nearby dark park. "That's Windy Hollow,"
Rachel said with a shiver.
"It won't be easy to
find them in there."

"Well, let's give it
our best shot," Trixie
replied with a bright
smile, flying into the
dark night. The two
friends slipped through
the park gate and into
the shadows after her. At once,
they could hear the wind that gave the
park its name. It rustled through the leaves
and put a chill in the air.

"It really feels like Halloween now,"
Kirsty whispered as she searched the inky
night for signs of the goblins. There were
no streetlights, and heavy clouds covered
the moon. The only light came from
their three fairy wands. The girls tiptoed
along, stopping every few steps to try and
listen for the goblins.

"*Shhhh*," Trixie warned them. "I think
we're close." The little fairy peeked over
the crest of a hill and motioned for Kirsty
and Rachel to stop. "They're down
there," she whispered. The girls got on
their hands and knees, and crawled up
the grassy slope to look over the hill.

Sure enough, the group of ghosts was
in the valley, rooting through the candy
stash again.

"If they have the magic candy corn,

they're bound to find it soon," Rachel said, worried.

"Not if we find it first," Kirsty replied. "Trixie, how do you feel about playing a little Halloween trick?" Kirsty's eyes brightened as she told Rachel and Trixie her plan.

"It's worth a try," Trixie said with a smirk. "I can't do much while the candy is missing, but I still have enough magic for a little trick!" She gave her wand a twirl and recited a spell:

The goblins think they're in disguise,
but now real ghosts are on the rise.
Raise those sheets up in the air.
Then all goblins should beware!

As soon as Trixie was done speaking, the sheets that covered the goblins lifted into the air. They floated just above the goblins' heads and looked like real ghosts!

Rachel and Kirsty gave each other a thumbs-up and then spoke in their spookiest voices. "*Oooooooo,*" they moaned.

"Give back the candy you stole. *Ooooooooooo!*"

At once, the goblins looked up and saw the sheets fluttering in the wind.

"Ghosts!" they screeched.

"*Ooooooo!* Give back the candy," the girls repeated. The three friends giggled. The goblins were cowering below the ghostly sheets, shaking with fear.

Just then, a single goblin yelled, "I found the magic candy corn!" He held his hand up in the air. "Hooray!"

Kirsty, Rachel, and Trixie exchanged worried glances. "What do we do now?" Kirsty whispered.

"Chase him!" Rachel said. But before the friends could get to their feet, they heard a loud yowl. They saw Moonlight the mischievous kitten, pounce onto the goblin's back.

"*Ouch!*" the goblin yelped, trying to swat Moonlight off.

The other goblins scattered in different directions until only the one remained. All at once, Moonlight jumped to the ground, and the last goblin darted away after his friends.

Moonlight looked right up at Trixie and the two girls. "Meow," the black kitten mewed softly. "Meow, meow, meow," he repeated before leaping into the shadows.

"It's the glitter candy!" Trixie exclaimed. "Moonlight is telling us that the goblin dropped it!" The three friends raced down the hill to where the kitten had been.

Sure enough, there was the magical candy corn on the ground, along with all of the other stolen treats.

"I can't wait to get this back to Fairyland," Trixie declared, lifting the candy corn up in the air. As soon as she touched it, it shrank to its original Fairyland size. "Then there will be candy for everyone!"

"And all of the candy will taste extra sweet," Kirsty added.

The clouds floated away and the moon brightened the night with a silvery light.

"We sure are lucky that Moonlight came along when he did," Rachel said.

"I'm off to Fairyland," Trixie said, nodding. "Let me send you back to your neighborhood, so you can trick-or-treat!" Trixie held up her wand, and a whirl of star-shaped fairy dust circled Rachel and Kirsty. The two girls waved to Trixie. The next thing they knew, they were back on Rachel's street.

The friends looked down the street to make sure no one had seen them. Then they grinned. "No more tricks for us tonight," Kirsty said.

Rachel nodded, holding up her bag and giggling. "Now I'm ready for some sweet treats!"

BOOK THREE

THE CARAMEL APPLE CRISIS

TABLE OF CONTENTS

HO-HUM HALLOWEEN

"Trick or treat!" Rachel and Kirsty said in chorus. They had been busy collecting candy since Trixie went back to Fairyland with the magic candy corn.

"We have lots of treats now," Kirsty said, looking in her bag. "I'll have to save some chocolate for my mom. She always wants me to share with her."

Rachel laughed. "My dad loves candy too. I got my sweet tooth from him," she admitted. Then she looked at her watch. "We can go to a few more houses before it's time to head to the town Halloween party."

Between ringing doorbells and greeting neighbors, Rachel and Kirsty stayed on the lookout for Trixie. They also watched for Moonlight, the clever kitten. After a few minutes, Rachel pulled out the invitation her parents had given her. There was a picture of a spooky old house on the front.

"The party's at a new place," Rachel explained. "It used to be on the other side of town, but my parents said we'd be able to walk this year. I'm pretty sure I know where this address is."

The girls walked along the sidewalk. As they got closer to the town party, there were clusters of kids and parents heading the same way. "This is it," Rachel announced, checking the address on the invitation one more time. She stared down the long path to the old Victorian house.

"Really?" Kirsty questioned. "This is that spooky house we passed the other day. I thought you said no one lived here."

Overhearing the girls, a man dressed as a mad scientist stopped and raised his lab goggles. "This is the old Pratt mansion," he said. "The town bought it, and they're turning it into a community center."

"So this is where the new community center will be," Rachel said. "My parents were part of the planning group, but they kept the location a secret so they could surprise me."

"Well, this is the first event here," the man replied. "We'll see how it goes." As he waved goodbye and walked down the curvy path, Kirsty noticed he was wearing glow-in-the-dark rubber gloves and an old lab coat.

Just then, the girls overheard a family walking up behind them. "It's too scary," a little girl said to her father, who picked her up in his arms.

"I don't want to go in there," she pleaded. The girl, dressed as a koala, buried her head in her father's shoulder and tried not to look.

Kirsty couldn't help agreeing with the little girl. "Even the trees are creepy," she said, noticing how the bare branches made long, fingerlike shadows. "It looks like that house has a lot of secrets."

"Not you, too!" Rachel giggled. "You'll feel a lot better once we find the magic caramel apple and bring back the Halloween spirit." She grabbed her friend's hand and pulled her down the path toward the old mansion.

HAUNTED HOUSE PARTY

Rachel and Kirsty gasped as they walked through the mansion door.

"The decorations are fantastic," Kirsty murmured.

Papier-mâché ghosts hovered in the air, and a giant spider web stretched from the floor to the ceiling. Bunches of orange and black balloons were tied to the grand staircase in the center of the first floor.

Next to a stone fireplace, a rock band was playing "Monster Mash." The musicians were all dressed as mummies, and music filled the house. A long table of food was right next to the grand staircase. Both girls noted that there were no caramel apples to be seen.

Before the friends could take it all in, Rachel's mom rushed up to them. "I'm so glad you're here," she said. "We need people to start playing games and dancing. No one seems to be having fun."

Rachel looked around and realized that everyone was just standing around, not talking or eating or laughing. She gave Kirsty a knowing look. No one would have any fun until the caramel apple was returned to Fairyland!

"We're happy to help, Mom," promised Rachel.

"Okay, how about you go to the third floor? That's where all the games are," Mrs. Walker said.

Kirsty looked up the tall staircase. It was like something out of an old movie.

"Let's start looking at the top and make our way down," she whispered to Rachel, who nodded. "The last piece of glitter candy might be here." Judging from the glum faces on all the party-goers, they needed to find the magic candy fast.

Once they climbed up to the third floor, the friends saw a long, narrow hallway. It was lined with bookshelves, and there were three dark wooden doors.

A sign for a different activity hung on each door. "Let's go to the pumpkin-carving room first," Rachel suggested.

As soon as they stepped inside, they heard a group of boys bickering. "Your costume is silly," one of the boys said. "We were supposed to dress up as something *green*."

"So? I'm Peter Pan," the other boy said.

"Peter Pan isn't green," another retorted. "He just *wears* green."

Rachel and Kirsty looked at each other in surprise. "They're goblins!" they whispered, realizing everyone in the group was wearing a green costume that matched their skin. One goblin was dressed as a bunch of grapes, and another was dressed as a turtle. The two goblins pestering Peter Pan were dressed as trees.

All at once, a cloud of star-shaped fairy dust showered over Rachel and Kirsty. "Trixie!" they called, excited to see their friend, who quickly ducked behind Rachel's hair.

"Look, Trixie," said Kirsty, pointing. "Goblins. If they're here, the missing magic caramel apple must be nearby too!"

"And they aren't alone," Trixie said softly. Then she motioned to a table in the corner where several kids had started carving pumpkins.

Rachel followed the fairy's gaze and gasped. There, sitting in the new Tippington Community Center, was Jack Frost!

Jack's Lantern

"*Brrr.* Just looking at him gives me the chills," Kirsty confessed.

There was something about Jack Frost's magic that made the air feel frigid whenever the troublemaker was around.

"I wonder what he's up to," Rachel said. "Let's find out."

The girls tiptoed
closer and hid
behind a stand-
up skeleton. To
their surprise,
Jack Frost
was carefully
carving a
mouth full of
crooked teeth
into his pumpkin.
He leaned back and
stared at the jack-o'-lantern.
He seemed very pleased with himself.

All at once, Jack Frost looked up and
glared around the room. He pushed his
seat back and strode over to the gang
of goblins. "What's going on here?" he
demanded. "I thought I told you that we

can't let the humans have all the fun. Now
get going and find that magic candy!"

"Well, that explains why he's here,"
said Kirsty.

"He wants to make sure they find the
caramel apple," Trixie said thoughtfully.
"Remember, just one bite from someone
who doesn't believe in Halloween, and there
won't be any Halloween spirit this year."

"Then we'd better hurry and find that apple first!" Rachel said. "My parents worked so hard on this center. I don't want the first party here to be ruined."

"What about your parents?" a voice said. The girls quickly turned around.

"Oh! Hi, Dad," Rachel gasped, brushing her hair forward to make sure Trixie was well hidden.

"I was just telling Kirsty how much fun I'm having. You all did a great job planning the party."

"Well, thanks," Mr. Walker said, lifting his cowboy hat. "I wish everyone was having as much fun as you. Could you help in the next room for a minute? I need someone to run the game while I get more prizes."

"Of course," Kirsty said, hoping Rachel's dad wouldn't notice the goblins or Jack Frost.

As soon as Mr. Walker left, the friends rushed to the room where a Musical Chairs sign was posted.

The girls looked around. There were about ten kids sitting on chairs in the middle of the room. They all looked bored. Most of the parents were leaning against the wall. "So, we need to start and stop the music," said Rachel, heading over to the stereo.

"And take a chair away each time," Kirsty said.

"And keep an eye out for goblins!" Trixie added. "Okay. Is everyone ready?" Rachel called out, but only a couple of kids nodded in response. "Here we go. Find a new seat when the music stops!" Then she pushed the PLAY button. As soon as the kids started to circle the empty seats, Jack Frost skipped into the room. He was holding his jack-o'-lantern, and it had a giant blue ribbon on it. "I won, I won," he sang, joining the kids who were playing musical chairs.

Kirsty looked on, completely shocked. "I guess I won't take a chair away," she said to Rachel, "since we have another player now." The best friends were used to trying to stay away from Jack Frost, but they couldn't exactly leave when they were in charge of the game!

Rachel nodded and pushed STOP. The kids all scrambled for a seat, and Jack Frost beat a child dressed as a ninja to the very last chair. He plopped

his pumpkin in his lap and
clapped his hands in
joy. No one seemed
to notice that Jack
Frost was not a
little kid. In fact,
he was acting
more like a kid
than any of the
kids in the room!
The ninja dragged
his feet as he headed
over to his father.

Just then, Rachel's dad
walked through the door with a bag
of puzzles, whistles, and other prizes.
"Thanks, girls," he said, placing the bag
next to the stereo on the table. "You
can go check out the other rooms if
you want."

At first, Rachel paused. She wondered if they should stay there and keep an eye on Jack Frost. Then a loud crash came from

the hallway, and she saw Moonlight skitter past the open door. A crowd of goblins, all in green, raced after him.

A HIDDEN KITTEN

"Thanks, Dad," Rachel said, giving him a quick smile. Then she and Kirsty ran out the door and after the goblins.

Almost immediately, the girls skidded to a stop. The goblins were huddled at the top of the staircase, each staring in a different direction.

"Where did that cat go?" the tallest goblin asked.

"It just disappeared," muttered one wearing a frog costume.

"It must be magic," guessed the Peter Pan goblin.

The goblins all looked confused, but then the goblin who was dressed as a bunch of grapes stamped his foot. "The cat could not have disappeared!" the goblin declared. "He just ran down the stairs before we could see him. Let's split up and find him. He showed up whenever we found the other candies, so he must know where the caramel apple is too!"

Kirsty and Rachel watched as the goblins ran down the stairs and then separated to search for the missing kitten.

Trixie peeked out from behind Rachel's hair. "It's true," she whispered. "It seems like Moonlight knew where to find the other magic candy. Maybe he can help us find the magic caramel apple."

"But first, we have to find him before the goblins do," Rachel pointed out.

Suddenly, Trixie raised a finger to her mouth. "Did you hear that?"

Rachel and Kirsty nodded. Then they heard it again . . . a tiny meow.

"It sounds like it came from behind there," said Rachel, pointing to a bookshelf lining the hallway.

Kirsty examined the bookshelf on the wall. "Look!" exclaimed Kirsty. "Maybe it did!"

One book appeared to be sticking out farther than the others. It was titled *The Secret Staircase*. As soon as Kirsty pulled

on the book's spine, the entire bookshelf slid to the side. There, sitting in the dark, was Moonlight. Behind him was a spiral staircase, almost impossible to see in the gloom.

"Meow, meow," the little cat said. He quickly turned around and disappeared down the mysterious staircase.

"He must want us to take this secret passageway," Trixie said. "Oh, what fun! Let's hurry."

Rachel and Kirsty looked at each other. It was one thing *finding* a hidden staircase, and another thing actually taking it. "I told you this house is full of secrets," Kirsty insisted.

"Come on!" Trixie said, flying into the dark stairwell. "How else will we save Halloween?" Trixie's wand started to glow, and the girls hurried after the fairy. The secret door slid shut behind them.

At once, the girls' wands began to glow as well. "I wonder how long it's been since someone was in here," Rachel wondered, plucking a cobweb from her hair.

The wooden stairs creaked with each step she took.

"I don't know," Trixie said, "but I'm sure Moonlight has a special plan."

Kirsty hoped so. She liked the idea of a secret passageway, but this one was spooky, dark, and dirty, and the stairs went in such a tight circle that she was getting dizzy!

The three friends carefully descended the gloomy staircase, looking for a hint that would help them find the last piece of glitter candy. But before they found any clues, they reached the bottom of the stairs.

"Okay then," Kirsty said. "Let's look for a way out."

"This looks like it might work," Rachel commented, pointing to a doorknob with a fancy flower design on it.

"I'll give it a try." She gave it a twist and a tug, and the door slid to the side with a crack.

As a sliver of light entered the dark stairwell, Rachel peeked out. "It's the party room on the main floor! No one sees us! This must be a secret door. We're right near the food table."

Trixie and Kirsty rushed over to have a look. Trixie hovered over Rachel's head, and Kirsty ducked beneath. "Yum!" said Kirsty. "I see popcorn, pretzels, apple cider,

pumpkin muffins, and all kinds of candy.
But I still don't see—"

"I see caramel apples!" Trixie declared.

"Oh!" Rachel exclaimed. "They must
have just set them out. I see them, too.
And the one in the middle has a bright
orange glitter wrapper!"

Just as Rachel said it, all three friends
gasped.

Someone was standing by the apples and
rubbing his hands together gleefully. That
someone was Jack Frost!

A FESTIVE FROST

"Oh no! He can't eat it!" Rachel yelled, but Kirsty stopped her from opening the door all the way.

"We need a plan," Kirsty explained.

"She's right," Trixie agreed. "If we go out there now, Jack Frost will spot us, grab the caramel apple, and we won't have a chance."

Just then, a little boy dressed as a pirate walked up to the food table, right next to Jack Frost. Jack Frost stretched his bony fingers toward the magic caramel apple.

"Shiver me timbers!" the young pirate bellowed suddenly, lifting up his eye patch for a better look. "I like your Jack Frost costume, matey. Did you make it yourself?"

The three friends hiding
behind the door were
surprised to see Jack
Frost blush. "Um,
well, my mother
made it," he said.

Rachel and
Kirsty looked at
each other and
giggled.

"It looks so real,"
the little boy said. "I
want to be Jack Frost
next year."

"You make a good pirate," Jack Frost
chuckled quietly. Then, without even
looking, he reached out and grabbed the
caramel apple with the glitter wrapper.

Trixie and the girls held their breath.

"Would you like this?" he asked the boy.

Rachel thought that Jack Frost was teasing the little pirate, but his smile looked genuine. Just as the boy was about to take the apple, a goblin ran up and snatched it from his hands. "I got it!" the goblin shrieked.

"What? No! It was for him!" Jack Frost cried, but the goblin didn't seem to notice that Jack Frost was even there. Just then, another goblin snatched the caramel apple away and held it up in the air.

"Hee, hee! Hooray for me!" the goblin hooted. "I'm going to give it to Jack Frost!" Then he took off, holding the apple in the air.

"What's happening?" Rachel asked. "Don't they know Jack Frost is right here?"

"I guess not!" Trixie laughed, shaking her head.

"We have to do something!" Kirsty declared.

"Let's wait and see what happens," Trixie advised.

Just then, the Peter Pan goblin leaped up and clutched the caramel apple. "It's mine now!" he yelled, running across the room.

The parents at the party rolled their eyes, assuming that the goblins were kids with horrible manners. The Peter Pan goblin cackled with joy as he ran, but he didn't watch where he was going. He tripped over a witch's broom and went sprawling forward. The magic caramel apple flew from his hands and up toward the ceiling.

Suddenly, Trixie, Rachel, and Kirsty

spotted Moonlight, perched on the chandelier. With a swat of his paw, Moonlight batted the caramel apple toward a bunch of balloons. The apple bounced right off them! Everyone at the party was trying to ignore the bratty goblins, so no one noticed the apple whiz over their heads and through a tiny, open crack in the secret door and right into Kirsty's outstretched hand.

"Wow! You caught it!" Rachel cried, gazing at Kirsty with excitement. "This time, the magic really did come to us!" she said with a laugh.

"Good catch!" Trixie exclaimed. "Thank you so much." The Halloween fairy beamed as she tapped the apple with her wand and it shrank back to its Fairyland size. "I guess Moonlight had a plan all along. Now I need to hurry back to Fairyland, so everyone can share in the magic of Halloween! I'll be back soon."

As Trixie disappeared in a whirl of fairy dust, Rachel and Kirsty slipped out the secret door and joined the party.

Rachel smiled. "I can't wait until Trixie gets the last piece of candy back to Fairyland."

"The party feels more fun already," Kirsty said, looking around. Then her eyes stopped on an unusual sight. Kirsty tugged Rachel's sleeve and pointed. Jack Frost was sitting in the corner with his young pirate friend, and they were both eating caramel apples.

"Hmm. Is it possible that he wasn't after the magic caramel apple after all?" Kirsty wondered.

Then she and her best friend looked each other in the eye. "No," they agreed, shaking their heads and giggling.

"And he's certainly not letting the people have all the fun. He's enjoying himself as much as anyone," Rachel admitted.

"Maybe Jack Frost just didn't want to be

left out of the magic of Halloween," suggested Kirsty.

The band started back up, and the dance floor filled with ghosts, ghouls, and goblins (some dressed as limes and Christmas trees). Rachel saw her parents laughing with a skeleton and a wizard.

Out of the corner of their eyes, the girls noticed a burst of glittery stars brighten the night sky. "Maybe it's Trixie," Kirsty said. The best friends rushed out the door and found Trixie on top of a round pumpkin.

"I wanted to come back and thank you," the fairy said. "And give you these pumpkin candy jars from the king and queen. They are so grateful for all of your help. Now everyone can have a happy Halloween!"

"Thank you, Trixie. We had a lot of fun," said Rachel, lifting the lid off her candy jar. It was filled with candy corn, chocolate bars, and caramel apples—all in orange glitter wrappers.

"This is so nice of you, Trixie," Kirsty added. "But are you sure that's the only reason you came back?"

All at once, a little black cat bounded from the shadows. As Moonlight leaped toward Trixie, he magically shrank to Fairyland size and landed in the fairy's lap.

"Oh, Moonlight!" Trixie said with glee. "Now this is the happiest Halloween of all!"

With that, the fairy and her kitten vanished in a shower of stars.

"I guess it's time to join the Halloween party," Rachel said, smiling at her friend.

"We should celebrate," Kirsty agreed. "We got to help our friends, the fairies, and there's nothing sweeter than that."

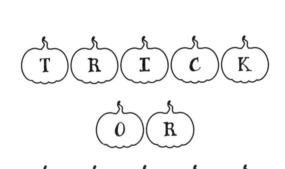

Did you find all twelve hidden letters? The special Halloween phrase is **Trick or Treat**!

Now it's time for Kirsty and
Rachel to help . . .

HOLLY ᴛʜᴇ CHRISTMAS FAIRY.

Read on for a sneak peek . . .

HOLLY
THE CHRISTMAS FAIRY

A Magical Mistake

"Only three days to go!" Rachel Walker said, sighing happily. She was attaching Christmas cards to long pieces of red ribbon, so that she could hang them on the living room wall. "I love Christmas! Don't you, Kirsty?"

Kirsty Tate, Rachel's best friend, nodded.

"Of course," she replied, handing Rachel another pile of cards. "It's a magical time of year!"

Rachel and Kirsty laughed and touched the golden lockets they both wore around their necks. The two girls shared a wonderful secret. No one else knew it, but they were friends with fairies!

Kirsty and Rachel had visited Fairyland when their fairy friends needed help. They had rescued the Rainbow Fairies after they were cast out of Fairyland by nasty Jack Frost.

In return for their help rescuing the fairies, the Fairy King and Queen had given Rachel and Kirsty each a gold locket. The lockets were full of magical fairy dust. The girls could use it to take them to Fairyland whenever they needed help from the fairies.

"Thanks for asking me to stay," said Kirsty, cutting another piece of ribbon. "Mom says she and Dad will pick me up on Christmas Eve."

"We might get some snow before then!" Rachel said, smiling. "The weather's getting much colder. I wonder what Christmas is like in Fairyland."

Just then, the door opened and Mrs. Walker came into the room. She was followed by Buttons, Rachel's friendly, shaggy dog. He was white with gray patches and had a long, furry tail.

"Oh, girls, that looks great!" Rachel's mom exclaimed when she saw the cards hanging on the walls. "We'll go over to Hillfield's Farm and pick out a Christmas tree tonight."

"Hooray!" Rachel cried. "Can Kirsty and I decorate it?"

"We were hoping you would!" Mrs. Walker laughed. "You can get the decorations out of the garage after lunch."

"Buttons seems to love Christmas too," Kirsty said, smiling. The dog was sniffing the cards and ribbons.

"He does," Rachel replied. "Every year, I buy him some doggie treats and wrap them up. And every year, hc finds them and eats them before Christmas!"

Buttons wagged his tail. Then he grabbed the end of a ribbon in his mouth, and ran off, trailing red ribbon behind him.

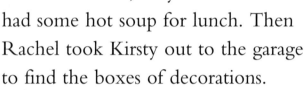

"Buttons, no!" Rachel yelled. She and Kirsty ran after him to get the ribbon back.

When the girls had finished hanging the Christmas cards, they had some hot soup for lunch. Then Rachel took Kirsty out to the garage to find the boxes of decorations.

"It's getting colder," Kirsty said, shivering. "Maybe it will snow!"

"I hope so," Rachel replied. She switched on the garage light. "The decorations are up there." She pointed at a shelf above the workbench. "I'll stand on the stepladder and hand the boxes down to you."

"OK," Kirsty agreed.

Rachel climbed up the ladder and began to pass the boxes down. They were full of silver stars, shiny tinsel, and glittering ornaments in pink, purple, and silver.

RAINBOW magic

More Titles to Read

RAINBOW FAIRIES 1–4

RAINBOW FAIRIES 5–7
+ BONUS PET FAIRY #1

PET FAIRIES 1–4

SPECIAL EDITION:
HOLLY THE CHRISTMAS FAIRY

☆ ☆ ☆ ☆ ☆ ☆ ☆

BEHIND THE MAGIC

DAISY MEADOWS is a pseudonym for the four writers of the internationally best-selling *Rainbow Magic* series: Narinder Dhami, Sue Bentley, Linda Chapman, and Sue Mongredien. *Rainbow Magic* is the no.1 bestselling series for children ages 5 and up with over 40 million copies sold worldwide!

GEORGIE RIPPER was born in London and is a children's book illustrator known for her work on the *Rainbow Magic* series of fairy books. She won the Macmillan Prize for Picture Book Illustration in 2000 with *My Best Friend Bob* and *Little Brown Bushrat*, which she wrote and illustrated.